Wizard Wig

First published in 2008
by Wayland

Text copyright © Anne Cassidy 2008
Illustration copyright © Martin Remphry 2008

Wayland
338 Euston Road
London NW1 3BH

Wayland Australia
Level 17/207 Kent Street
Sydney, NSW 2000

Series Editor: Louise John
Cover design: Paul Cherrill
Design: D.R.ink
Consultant: Shirley Bickler

A CIP catalogue record for this book is available from the British Library.

ISBN 9780750251891

Printed in China

Wayland is a division of Hachette Children's Books,
an Hachette Livre UK Company

www.hachettelivre.co.uk

Wizard Wig

Written by Anne Cassidy
Illustrated by Martin Remphry

WAYLAND

Wizzle the wizard was casting
a spell.

"I command you to become a
magic mirror!"

"Whoever looks into this mirror will be beautiful!" Wizzle said.
The queen looked into the mirror.

"No!" cried out Wizzle's sister, Wanda.

But it was too late. Wizzle's spell
had gone badly wrong – again!
The queen began to sob.

Later, the king came to
Wizzle's room.

"Where is my wizard?" he shouted.

"Look," the king cried, "I'm losing my hair – it's all falling out. Soon I'll have no hair left!"

"I have a spell which makes hair grow," said Wizzle.

Wanda took an old spell book from the shelf.

"Get me a unicorn's horn, some fairy wings and... a dragon's egg! That should do it," said Wizzle, and he mixed everything together.

Wizzle put the mixture onto the king's head.

He whispered some magic words.
"Izzle, Wizzle, Woo!"

The king's head fizzed and sparkled.
His hair began to grow longer,
thicker and fluffier. He even had
curls and ringlets!

It grew so much that it reached
the floor.
"Make it stop," the king cried.
"Stop it at once!"

Wizzle didn't know what to do!
He didn't know how to stop it.

He picked up a jug of water and threw it over the king's head.

The king's hair fell out.
He was completely bald!

The king was furious. His face
turned red. He shook his fist.

"You are the worst wizard in the
world. Get out of my castle!"

Wizard Wizzle left the castle.
He felt very sad.

"Don't worry," Wanda shouted, "I'll think of a way to get you back in the castle."

Inside the castle, Wanda saw a
servant weaving.

She was making a beautiful piece
of cloth.

Wanda had an idea. She told the servant what she wanted to do.

The servant smiled.

That night Wanda crept into the king's bedroom, while he was asleep.

She measured his head with a tape measure.

The next morning, Wizzle came
to see the king.

"Please give me one more chance!"
he said. "I have found the best spell
ever to make new hair."

"I have hair from a lion's mane, some feathers from a golden eagle and some diamond dust."

Wizzle sprinkled them over a box.

"Izzle, Wizle, Woo! The king must have beautiful hair!" he whispered.

Wanda lifted the lid. Inside there was a wig.

"This is fantastic," said the king.
"I really love it!"

"Maybe you're not such a bad wizard after all," he said, smiling at Wizzle.